**For Max
and Sam
and Ian**

ALADDIN · An imprint of Simon & Schuster Children's Publishing Division · 1230 Avenue of the Americas, New York, New York 10020 · First Aladdin hardcover edition June 2017 · Copyright © 2017 by Andrew Bergmann · All rights reserved, including the right of reproduction in whole or in part in any form. · ALADDIN and related logo are registered trademarks of Simon & Schuster, Inc. · For information about special discounts for bulk purchases, please contact Simon & Schuster Special Sales at 1-866-506-1949 or business@simonandschuster.com. · The Simon & Schuster Speakers Bureau can bring authors to your live event. For more information or to book an event contact the Simon & Schuster Speakers Bureau at 1-866-248-3049 or visit our website at www.simonspeakers.com. · Book designed by Laura Lyn DiSiena · The illustrations for this book were rendered digitally. · The text of this book was set in Filosofia · Manufactured in China 0317 SCP · 2 4 6 8 10 9 7 5 3 1 · Library of Congress Control Number 2016962340 · ISBN 978-1-4814-9100-6 (hc) · ISBN 978-1-4814-9101-3 (eBook)

THE STARRY GIRAFFE

Written and illustrated by **ANDY BERGMANN**

ALADDIN
New York   London   Toronto   Sydney   New Delhi

The starry giraffe stumbled
upon a plump apple tree.

She was very hungry.

The giraffe searched for
the most delicious-looking apple
and plucked it off.

Just when she opened up to take
a big bite, a little brown mouse
popped out of his hole.

"I'm very hungry," he squeaked,
"but I am much too little to reach
those delicious apples."

"Here you go," said the giraffe.

"Thank you," said the mouse as he moused back into his hole.

The starry giraffe turned to find
the second-most-delicious apple
on the tree.

She picked a round, rosy red one
that smelled so good, she could
just about taste it.

When she just about tasted it,
a family of skunks scurried up.

The giraffe presented them each with an apple. The excited skunk family jumped all about.

All this apple picking made
the starry giraffe quite tired.

An old gray bunny thumped up.
The giraffe gave him an apple.

A raccoon followed.
One apple for him.

The snake got two.

And a rhino carried one off
in his lunch box to eat later.

The starry giraffe was hungrier
than ever. Only one lonely apple
remained on the tree.

She looked around to see if anyone
else might arrive. It was all quiet.

The giraffe stretched
up high and picked
the last apple.

Then she noticed a tiny inchworm
staring up with a hungry face.

Worms quite enjoy apples,
so she gave him the final one.

The giraffe's stomach rumbled.
She felt tired and a little sad.

After a few moments of rest,
the starry giraffe stood up tall.

She walked to the next tree
and ate twenty-seven apples.